THE Princess IN BLACK

Shannon Hale & Dean Hale

illustrated by
LeUyen Pham

SCHOLASTIC INC.

ISBN 978-0-545-81245-0

Text copyright © 2014 by Shannon and Dean Hale. Illustrations copyright © 2014 by LeUyen Pham. All rights reserved. Published by Scholastic Inc., 557 Broadway, New York, NY 10012, by arrangement with Candlewick Press. SCHOLASTIC and associated logos are trademarks and/or registered trademarks of Scholastic Inc.

12 11   18 19 20/0

Printed in the U.S.A.   40

First Scholastic paperback printing, September 2015

This book was typeset in Kennerly.
The illustrations were done in watercolor and ink.

For our own Princess Magnolia
S. H. and D. H.

To Luna, Emilie, Julia, Angelique, and Deniz —
my little group of supercool princesses
L. P.

Chapter 1

Princess Magnolia was having hot chocolate and scones with Duchess Wigtower. The hot chocolate was hot. The scones were sweet. The breeze from the window was warm and wishy.

"How lovely of you to visit," said Princess Magnolia. "And unexpected."

"I love to meet people in their own homes," said Duchess Wigtower. "I always uncover secrets."

"Secrets?" said Princess Magnolia.

"Yes, secrets," said Duchess Wigtower. "Hidden messes, skeletons in closets, that sort of thing."

"Closets?" said Princess Magnolia. The hot chocolate burned her lip. The breeze knocked her curls into her face. She was no longer enjoying herself.

"You seem so prim and perfect." Duchess Wigtower leaned forward. "But everyone has a secret."

Princess Magnolia brushed crumbs off her frilly pink dress. She hoped she didn't look nervous. Because she did indeed have a secret. A huge secret. A secret she didn't want anyone to uncover. Especially not the nosy duchess.

Just then, Princess Magnolia's glitter-stone ring rang.

The monster alarm, thought Princess Magnolia. *Not now!*

"What was that ringing sound?" asked Duchess Wigtower.

"A bird?" said Princess Magnolia.

She wished her ring's ring sounded anything like a bird. It didn't.

"Strange bird," said the duchess.

"Maybe it's sick," said Princess Magnolia. "I should check."

Princess Magnolia minced to the door. Her glass slippers went *tink-tink-tink-tink*.

"You're going to just leave me here?" said the duchess.

"I'll hurry back!" said Princess Magnolia.

She smiled sweetly. She shut the door softly.

And then Princess Magnolia ran.

Chapter 2

Princesses do not run.

Princesses do not stuff frilly pink dresses into broom closets.

Princesses do not wear black.

And princesses most definitely do not slide down secret chutes and high-jump castle walls.

But then, most princesses do not live near an entrance to Monster Land.

Stopping monsters was no job for prim and perfect Princess Magnolia. But fortunately Princess Magnolia did have a secret.

She was secretly the Princess in Black! And stopping monsters was the perfect job for the Princess in Black.

Chapter 3

In the courtyard, Frimplepants was nibbling an apple. He swished his sparkly tail. He pranced on his golden hooves. He gave the horn upon his brow a little toss.

Clearly, Frimplepants was a unicorn. Or was he?

Frimplepants's glitter-stone horse-shoe rang. The monster alarm!

He took three dainty steps toward the castle wall.

He looked right. He looked left.

No one was watching. So Frimplepants entered a secret passage.

Horn lifted off. Golden hooves slid aside.

Sparkly mane and tail shook free.

He came out the other side. He was no longer Frimplepants the unicorn. He was Blacky, the Princess in Black's faithful pony!

Just then, the Princess in Black was soaring over the castle wall. She landed on Blacky's back.

"Fly, Blacky, fly!" she said. "To the goat pasture, as fast as you can. There's a nosy duchess in the castle."

They charged through the forest. Birds flapped out of their way.

The birds squawked. The birds cheeped. The birds sounded nothing like a ringing ring.

Chapter 4

The big blue monster was hungry. Monster Land was full of monsters. Some were small. Some were big. Some were bigger than the big blue monster. They were always eating up the good food.

There was a hole in the ceiling of Monster Land. The smell of goats floated in through the hole. Shaggy goats. Plump goats. Delicious goats. The big blue monster began to drool.

Wasn't there a rule against climbing through that hole? Yes, there was. But the monster couldn't remember why.

Was it because the sun was too shiny up there?

Was it because the air was unpleasantly fresh?

No, there had been some other reason. . . .

The big blue monster was too hungry to remember. It climbed through the hole.

Chapter 5

Duff the goat boy was not part goat and part boy. That would have been interesting. But Duff was just a boy who took care of goats.

He quite liked goats. They had honey-brown eyes. They had floppy ears. They made snuffling noises.

Duff did not like goat-eating monsters.

A blue arm reached out of the hole.

"Not another one," said Duff. He picked up his crook.

A blue monster emerged.

It was big.

The monster roared. It was loud.

Duff dropped his crook. His knees shook.

"H-h-help!" he croaked.

In the distance, a pony neighed.

Chapter 6

The Princess in Black galloped into the goat pasture. A big blue monster was holding a goat in each paw. It opened its mouth as wide as it would go. Which was very wide.

"Not so fast!" said the Princess in Black.

Blacky galloped toward the big tree. The Princess in Black grabbed a branch. She swung from her pony's back. She landed in the tree.

"Why did you come here?" asked the Princess in Black.

"EAT GOATS," said the big blue monster.

"You may not eat the goats," she said.

"EAT GOATS!" hollered the big blue monster.

"You may *not* eat the goats!" she said again. "Behave, beast!"

The big blue monster set down the goats near a small tree. It tore the tree from the ground.

The Princess in Black did a backflip onto the grass. She pushed a switch on her scepter. It turned into a staff.

The big blue monster roared and swung the tree. The staff met it.

SPARKLE
SLAM!

The Princess in Black and the big blue monster waged battle.

PRINCESS POUNCE!

BLACKY BUCK!

With luck, the battle would be quick. Duchess Wigtower was in Princess Magnolia's castle. Her castle was full of secrets. Especially the broom closet. The Princess in Black hoped the duchess would not snoop.

Chapter 7

The duchess began to snoop.

Princess Magnolia's tower was spotless. The windows were as clear as glass. The couches were as soft as cushions. It was almost *too* perfect. Something must be amiss.

Duchess Wigtower opened a closet. Frilly pink dresses. Perfect for a princess. She opened drawers. White gloves and flowered headbands. Beaded handkerchiefs and crystal bracelets.

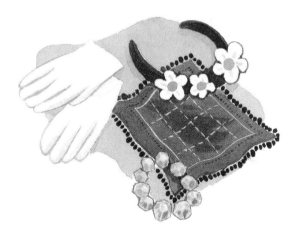

All perfect for a princess.

"Drat," said the duchess. "No one is this perfect."

The duchess was determined to un-cover a secret in Princess Magnolia's castle. She just had to look harder.

Chapter 8

Duff the goat boy settled onto a tree stump. He always enjoyed the Princess in Black's ninja skills. But today he noticed something new. The Princess in Black reminded him of Princess Magnolia.

Without her mask, they might even look the same. The Princess in Black was the same height as Duff. So was Princess Magnolia.

The Princess in Black had honey-brown eyes. So did Princess Magnolia.

The Princess in Black had a sparkly tiara. So did Princess Magnolia.

Could the two princesses be the same girl?

But Princess Magnolia wore glass
slippers on weekdays. Princess Magnolia was afraid of snails. Sunlight
made Princess Magnolia sneeze.

And at the moment, the Princess
in Black was hog-tying a monster.

Duff laughed at his silly imagination. He nibbled some popcorn. He waited for the part when he would cheer.

Chapter 9

The duchess peeked under a table. Not so much as a wad of gum! Was Princess Magnolia as perfect as she seemed? No, surely everyone had secrets. Duchess Wigtower would find *something* amiss.

The duchess left Princess Magnolia's tower room. She poked around the throne room.

She examined the ballroom.

She explored the kitchen. She even paused to inspect the cookies.

Everything was completely perfect.

Then she noticed a broom closet. Something was stuck beneath the door. She yanked it free.

A pair of coal-black stockings.

"Aha!" said the duchess.

Black stockings! Everyone knows that princesses don't wear black. Princess Magnolia did indeed have a secret.

Duchess Wigtower's frown turned into a crooked smile.

Chapter 10

The Princess in Black was trying not to worry about the nosy duchess. She was busy battling a big blue beast.

The monster was just so huge. And heavy. It was all tied up. But she couldn't push it back in the hole.

"Go back in that hole," said the Princess in Black.

"ROAR!" said the big blue monster.

"Behave, beast!" said the Princess in Black.

"ROOAARR!" said the big blue monster.

The Princess in Black sighed. She raised an eyebrow.

"Please," she said.

The big blue monster sighed, too. It rolled into the hole.

Duff cheered.

The Princess in Black bowed.

"Thank you, my friend. Until next time!"

She patted a goat's head. She sprang onto Blacky's back. They galloped into the forest.

She had to get back to Duchess Wigtower. She hoped she wasn't too late.

Chapter 11

The big blue monster plopped down
into Monster Land. It chewed off the
rope. The rope was pretty yummy.
But not as yummy as goats.

There was a rule not to climb through the hole. Now it remembered why.

The sun *was* too shiny up there. The air *was* unpleasantly fresh. But that had nothing to do with the rule.

Monsters should not climb through the hole because of the Princess in Black. She would not let them eat goats.

The big blue monster was going to remind the other monsters about the rule. But then it found a pile of toe-nail clippings.

"YUM," it said. And it forgot all about the Princess in Black.

Chapter 12

Duff whistled as he walked his goats home. No goats had been eaten. That meant it had been a good day.

All thanks to the Princess in Black.

He wished he could help her. But everyone knows that goat boys do not fight monsters.

He thought again about Princess Magnolia possibly being the Princess in Black. What a clever disguise that would be! No one would suspect a girl in glass slippers.

But of course, it was a silly idea.

If the goats stood up on their hind legs, they would be the same height as Duff. Just like the Princess in Black.

His goats had honey-brown eyes. Just like the Princess in Black. (None of them had tiaras, though.)

A goat would also be an excellent disguise for the Princess in Black!

No one would suspect a goat.

Just as no one would suspect a goat boy.

Duff was getting an idea.

Chapter 13

Duff's idea made him smile as he fed the goats. He smiled as he tugged on their nightshirts. He smiled as he kissed them good night.

And then Duff the goat boy got to work.

Goat boys do not get ideas.

Goat boys do not fashion masks and capes out of old goat blankets.

And goat boys most definitely do not make monster alarms out of goat bells and rope.

But then, most goat boys are not the Goat Avenger in disguise.

Duff would exercise. Duff would practice. And perhaps someday, the Goat Avenger would fight beside the Princess in Black. Look out, monsters!

Chapter 14

The Princess in Black high-jumped the castle wall. She crawled up the secret chute. Going up was much slower than going down.

There were three spiders in the chute. There were two bats. Even worse, there was one very cheeky snail. But the Princess in Black was not afraid.

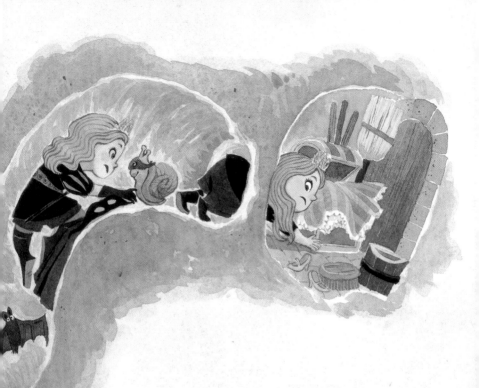

The tunnel ended in the broom
closet.

When she emerged from the closet,
she was no longer the Princess in
Black.

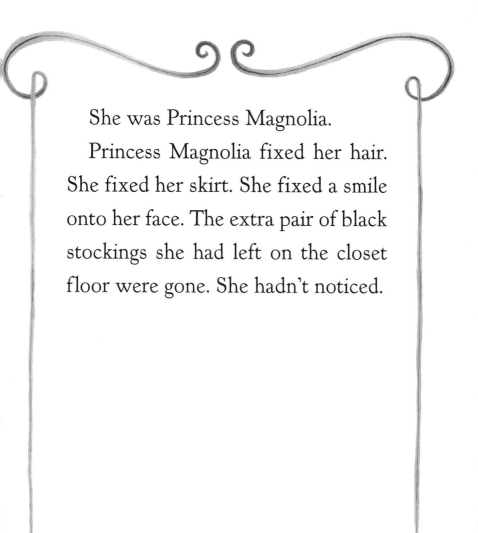

She was Princess Magnolia.

Princess Magnolia fixed her hair. She fixed her skirt. She fixed a smile onto her face. The extra pair of black stockings she had left on the closet floor were gone. She hadn't noticed.

Chapter 15

Princess Magnolia minced into her tower room.

"So sorry to keep you waiting," said Princess Magnolia. "All the birds are well and properly tweeting."

Duchess Wigtower took a long sip of cold hot chocolate. She smiled.

"While you were gone, I toured your castle," said the duchess.

Princess Magnolia froze. "You did?"

"Mm-hm," said the duchess. "And I discovered something in the broom closet."

Princess Magnolia gulped. "You did?"

"Yes," said the duchess. "These black stockings. I uncovered your secret!"

Princess Magnolia gasped. "You did?"

"Princess Magnolia, these white stockings are so filthy, they've turned as black as coal! You really must wash them. Everyone knows princesses don't wear black."

"Of course not!" said Princess Magnolia. "How clever of you."

Princess Magnolia smiled. She knew at least one princess who did wear black. But that would remain her secret.